BOYS ARE AMAZING!

SHORT STORIES FOR BOYS ABOUT SELF-ESTEEM, CONFIDENCE, AND INNER-STRENGTH | PRESENT FOR BOYS

David Wilson

ISBN – 9798495143159

THIS BOOK BELONGS TO

____

TABLE OF CONTENTS

CHAPTER 1: FIELD TRIP TO THE CRETACEOUS

Jack sat quietly at the back of the school bus. It was much noisier than normal; everyone was excited after the field trip to the museum. A couple of other boys sat near him, Reece and Fraser, were throwing balls of paper around. Jack sighed, popped on his headphones, and pulled out a new book on dinosaurs he'd bought at the museum shop as Mrs Cook, their teacher, came to the back of the bus. He flicked through the glossy pages, remembering how wonderful it had been seeing the fossils earlier that day. It was a shame he couldn't have spent longer looking at them. He had almost asked to, but he hadn't had the courage to speak up.

Suddenly, Jack felt sleepy. He closed his eyes and drifted to sleep. The bus lurched as if it had driven over a speed bump too quickly and their driver pulled up sharply, waking Jack. He was about to settle back into his nap but glanced up when he realised that the bus had grown quiet. He pulled out his earphones. Mrs Cook was reassuring Reece and Fraser that everything was fine, but she didn't sound convinced. Jack looked around and realised there were only the four of them on the bus. What was going on?

"What happened?" Reece asked. "Where did everyone go?"

Everyone seemed to be panicking. Everyone that was except Jack. He had noticed something outside the window. A plant. A very unusual plant. He squinted at it through the fog.

"Now, we should stay with the bus until we can be located, but it would help if we could get a phone signal. If any of you have a mobile, please check if you have reception," Mrs Cook said. Jack checked, but he had no reception. "Well, I'll go a little way up the road and see if I get any."

"I'll come," Jack said suddenly, almost surprising himself. He was always quiet, but he wanted to see the plant. It looked familiar.

Mrs Cook looked a little shocked that he'd spoken up, but also a tiny bit relieved.

"We'll come too," volunteered Fraser.

"Yeah. We should stick together," added Reece.

The four stepped out of the bus and into the swirling fog. They started to walk up a slight incline, keeping track of which way they went on Reece's compass and checking for a signal as they went. Jack was more interested in the plants, though.

"Cycads," he mumbled.

"What?" Reece asked.

"Mrs Cook," Jack said, his voice wavering a little.

"Yes?" she replied.

"These are cycads. Lots of them."

"Very good Jack. Maybe you'll be a botanist," she said with a smile.

"Palaeobotanist," he replied. "We haven't had these cycads here since the Cretaceous period."

Mrs Cook looked confused, but both Reece and Fraser looked unconcerned. A loud crashing sound a good way off spooked them all a little. Mrs Cook looked around frantically, then ushered them back the way they'd come. The fog had lifted a little now, so Jack could clearly see around him. Something large moved in the tree line, and a crested head lifted out of the bushes. The creature's eyes fell on the group, but they were smaller than it was and it lazily grabbed more plants and started chewing, unconcernedly. Jack stared at the creature in awe. Mrs Cook screeched.

"What is that?" Reece asked.

"Parasaurolophus!" Jack replied. He reached a hand out as if he was going to touch it, but Mrs Cook pulled him back, her eyes wide.

"It's OK, Mrs Cook," Jack said. "It's a herbivore. That crest on the back of its head makes a sort of echo that helps keep predators away. This is so awesome!"

Mrs Cook did not look convinced. Reece and Fraser just stared in surprise while Jack inched closer, looking over the great beast.

“H-h-how?” stammered Mrs Cook.

“I don’t know,” Jack replied. “But we should get back to the bus. If I had to guess, I’d say we somehow drove into the past.”

“Like time travelled to the Jurassic?” Fraser asked.

“Cretaceous,” Jack corrected.

“So, we don’t have to worry about T-Rex and those velociraptor things?” Reese asked.

Jack sighed and rubbed his head. "T-Rex, yes, they are from the Cretaceous. Velociraptors were the size of turkeys, so probably not."

Fraser and Reece exchanged glances, and Mrs Cook looked a little ill. Jack took her arm, and they started to walk quickly back towards the bus.

They got back onto the empty bus and sat down. Mrs Cook kept nervously glancing out of the window while Jack attempted to take photos. Fraser sat looking guilty until Reese elbowed him.

"Dude, you got to tell Mrs Cook," he said.

"Tell me what?" Mrs Cook asked.

"Fraser took something from the museum," Reece said. Fraser punched him in the arm, looking guilty. He sighed and pulled out a rock from his bag. It was strangely glowing purple.

"Wow!" he said. "Miss, it wasn't purple before!"

Jack scooted over to Fraser and stared at the rock. It was so bright it almost hurt his eyes to look at it.

"You think this is what caused this?" Reece asked.

"Maybe," Mrs Cook replied. "We should take it back. Maybe if we put it back, we can get home."

"But the museum is gone," Reece pointed out. "Or I guess, isn't here yet."

“Then we’ll put it where the museum should be,” Mrs Cook replied. “We didn’t go very far.”

“But Miss, there are, like, dinosaurs out there,” Reece pointed out. “Should we take the bus?”

Jack looked out at all the plants around them. It didn’t look like they’d be able to drive through them. Mrs Cook must have thought the same because she shook her head.

“Jack?” Jack looked up at his teacher. “You know a lot about this period. You’ll keep us safe.”

Jack gulped but nodded. They stepped out of the bus and began to walk back towards the museum. As they pushed their way through the abundant plant life, Jack heard a strange noise and glanced upward.

“Pterosaurs.” He pointed, and the others looked. “We’d better stay in the tall plants.”

They kept themselves surrounded by plants and kept walking slowly. Jack led the way and Mrs Cook took the rear.

“Look!” Fraser hissed. They all looked at the rock in his hands. It wasn’t glowing as much as it had before. “That’s good, right?”

“Probably,” said Reece.

The rock was almost back to its normal colour when they heard an odd, low rumbling coming from somewhere not too far away. Jack stopped suddenly, very worried.

"What is that?" Reece asked.

"T-Rex," Jack replied. "Keep moving, but go quietly."

"What! Don't they, like, roar?" Fraser asked.

"No. New studies suggest they made quieter, lower sounds. They also have an amazing sense of smell," Jack said.

"Great," muttered Reece.

Two things seemed to happen at once then. Firstly, a T-Rex lifted its enormous head out of the undergrowth close by. Jack pulled out his phone to snap a shot of it. Then, right at the same moment, the rock stopped glowing. Fraser immediately put it down, and a stunningly bright light erupted from it, blinding everyone, including the T-Rex.

Jack woke up on the school bus with a start. It was a dream, just a dream. He breathed a deep sigh of relief until he glanced at Reece. He and Fraser beamed at him and gave him a thumbs up. It was a dream, wasn't it? He pulled out his phone. The last image on it was very blurry, but he could just see the outline of a head, sharp, pointed teeth, and two intense eyes. Jack sat back in his seat, still not sure what had just really happened. What do you think? Did he really see a T-Rex?

CHAPTER 2: A GOOD DEED

Mike walked down the road towards his favourite bookshop. He was hoping to get the latest adventure of *Morgan's Magic*. It was so cool how Morgan had powers and could help people and defend the castle against evil. Mike turned the corner and stopped. The shop had a huge closed sign on its door. Mike sighed; he would have to wait another week to get his book now. Then he noticed a shop he'd never seen before across the street. It seemed to be filled with odd items, including bottles, herbs, and crystals. At first, he was just going to walk away, but then, in the window, he saw an advert for *Morgan's Magic*. They sold the book. Mike hurried across the road, his backpack bouncing as he went. Just as he was about to open the door, a man came rushing out.

"Stop, thief!" yelled an old man from behind the counter.

Mike didn't think. He stuck out his foot, and the man tripped over it, sprawling onto the pavement. The man dropped everything he had stolen, but scrambled to his feet and ran off. The old shopkeeper hobbled up to Mike, who had started to pick up the things on the floor.

"Thank you," said the old man.

"That's OK," Mike smiled. "I'm just sorry I didn't stop him."

“You tried, that is worth more,” the old man said. “Come on in. How can I help you?”

“Do you have *Morgan’s Magic*?” Mike asked. The old man smiled, his blue eyes lighting up.

“I do.” He pulled a copy of the book out from behind the counter.

“Brilliant. It’s the best book ever! I wish I was like Morgan,” Mike said, putting his money on the counter as he excitedly took the book.

“Oh, I don’t think I’d like that kind of power all the time, but I bet it would be fun for, oh I don’t know, a day maybe?” the man replied.

"Yeah, imagine that." Mike smiled.

The old man squinted at him a little, nodded, and then smiled. "I think a special reward for you, for helping me."

The old man picked up a plain leather bookmark and handed it to Mike with a smile. Mike waved it at him a little and said thank you before heading home.

Later that night, Mike snuggled down under his bed covers and read a few chapters of the book. When he felt tired, he pulled out the bookmark he had been given by the old man and popped it into the book, setting it down on the bedside table. He didn't see the strange golden light that shone from the bookmark, nor did he see the gold writing that seeped through the leather.

Mike woke up late the next morning and had to rush to get ready for school. He grabbed his book and threw it into his bag without even looking at it. The bus was just about to pull away when Mike rushed out of the door. He held his hand up, yelling "Wait!" He didn't expect anything to happen, but surprisingly, the bus stopped. Mike ran and clambered in through the open door. It was odd, though. The bus driver almost looked frozen until Mike stepped inside the bus. He shrugged it off and took a seat. He started to pull his book out of his bag, but before he had a chance to open it, he saw Ella, a girl from his class, accidentally knock her art project from her chair. Ella gasped in horror, and Mike reached out to try to catch it.

Just as he thought it would hit the floor and break, it seemed to stop falling and landed softly instead.

"Wow, that was lucky," someone said as Ella scooped it up. Mike looked around, confused.

At school, Mike met up with his friend Eric and told him about everything that had happened that morning.

"Weird," said Eric. "You think it's some kind of paranormal thing? Like a ghost."

"No." Mike shook his head. "It's odd, though."

"Did you get the book?" Eric asked.

"Yeah," Mike said, smiling. He pulled the book out and handed it to Eric.

"Cool bookmark. Why does it have a gold clock on it?" Eric asked.

Mike looked over Eric's shoulder at the bookmark. Sure enough, there was an elaborate golden clock printed on the leather.

"Hey, it has the right time," Eric pointed out. Mike was busy reading what it said underneath, though.

"Eric, read the writing," Mike said.

"One good turn deserves another, from one eight to the other. Magic at your fingertips, until away the time slips," Eric read. "What does that mean?"

"I think maybe I have magic until the clock reaches eight," Mike said.

"Don't be daft," Eric laughed. "Go on then, do some magic."

"What?" Mike asked.

"Looks like rain and we have gym first period. Make it sunny," Eric said. He adjusted his backpack and led the way towards the changing rooms.

"OK," Mike said. "Clouds go away, make it a sunny day."

Nothing happened, and Eric laughed as he pulled open the gym door. As the door closed behind them, a breeze blew up, rolling the grey clouds quickly across the sky. By the time Eric and Mike came out for PE, the sun was blazing. Eric looked at Mike.

For the next hour, they tested out the magic in little ways. They got the ball during a football match. They made one of the girls drop her hockey stick and even made Mr Fielding, their awful gym teacher, fall over his own feet. At break time, they sat together and wondered what to do.

"It should be something big," said Eric.

"What, like world peace?" asked Mike.

"I don't think you have that much magic," Eric replied.

"What then?" Mike asked.

"Don't know," Eric said. They sat in silence for a while, watching the children run around. The little kids from the primary school next door were out playing, too. One of them was a bit too high on the climbing frame. Suddenly, he slipped. Mike shouted and, just like Ella's artwork, he landed softly without getting hurt. Both Mike and Eric sighed in relief.

"Shame you can't magic them a safer playground and us one too. All we have is that old swing and a set of monkey bars I could reach from the floor when I was eight," Eric said with a sigh.

"Why not? It's not that big a bit of magic!" Mike mused.

"Go on then, give it a try," Eric said.

"Right," said Mike. "Magic us up a nice new swing, slides, that sort of thing!"

Nothing happened. Eric looked a little sad. "Maybe it wore off."

Just then, the bell rang and everyone filed inside for class. They were sitting at their desks doing their maths work when the headmaster, Mr Fry, came in to talk to their teacher.

"Morning, Miss Price," he said. "Morning class."

"Morning, sir," they chorused.

"I have good news for you all. I don't know if you remember, but we applied to get some money to refurbish the playing field, get some new goalposts and things. Well, it seems we got a lot more than we expected, so we're dividing the rest of the money to get you and the primary children some new playground equipment. I was hoping your class could give us some inspiration. Pictures and short notes on the things they'd like, that sort of thing," Mr Fry said.

Eric looked over at Mike, his mouth hanging open. Mike stared back, not sure what to say.

"Eric Gordon, close your mouth. You're not a guppy," Mr Fry said as he left.

For the rest of the day, Mike and Eric tried to do nice, small things around the school. Eric did suggest they wish for gold, or maybe for more magic powers, but Mike didn't think that sounded like a good idea. He felt somehow that he should only use his magic to help people and maybe to have the odd small treat. He wished the younger children could get extra outdoor time since Eric said his little sister Charlotte would like it, and it was announced that the primary school would be part of the forest school rotation from now on.

They wished that they could have a night off homework, or at least off doing a lot of it, and were rewarded with being asked to do the drawings or notes for the playground as their only homework. Eric wished they had jelly for lunch and they did – red, his favourite. Mike wished that they had better books in the library, and shortly afterwards, they saw new books being delivered. On top of the box, they could see a copy of *Morgan's Magic*.

At the end of the day, Mike asked if Eric could come over for tea and his mother agreed. Mike used his magic to wish they had the best tea ever. His father rang to say he had been given a huge contract at work and they could have takeout pizza and ice cream! Later that night, Eric and Mike sat watching a film together, scooping ice cream out of their bowls.

"It's kind of sad it has to end, really," Eric said.

"Maybe it won't," Mike said. "Not really. I mean, I got the magic because I did something good and it worked because we only wanted nice, small things and helped others. Maybe if we only do nice things and always try to help others, the magic will stay."

"Hope so," said Eric, taking another spoonful. Mike smiled.

CHAPTER 3: NEIGHBOURHOOD CLEAN UP

Jason rushed down the skatepark ramp with so much speed everything looked blurred. It was his favourite thing to do on a Saturday, grab his board and ride around the concrete ramps as fast as he could. He waved at his friend Maya, who was watching from a bench, and she waved back. He wondered why she wasn't skating today. Flipping up his board, he wandered over to her.

"Not riding today?" he asked.

"No. My Grammy is coming over. Mum said if I brought my board, I'd forget the time and not get back for tea." She giggled, and Jason laughed.

"You can take mine for a spin," he offered.

"Thanks, but I really should get back," Maya said.

"Sure?" he asked.

"OK, just one go. I can take the shortcut back over the playing fields," she said with a smile.

They spent a while taking turns on his board and chatting until Maya glanced at her watch and panicked.

"I am so late. I got to go. Thanks, Jason." She smiled and rushed off towards the playing fields, her blonde hair bouncing as she ran.

Jason carried on skating. He heard sirens a little while later, but he didn't think much of it. After all, this close to town, there were often the odd sirens going off. As dusk fell, he headed home. Arriving at his house, he pulled open the door and placed his board on the porch.

"Mum, I'm home," he called as he pulled off his helmet and knee pads.

He was surprised when his mum came to the door. She looked unhappy. "Jason, I'm glad you're back. Mrs Wheeler called. Maya had an accident."

Jason felt himself go cold. “What happened? Is she OK?”

His mum nodded. “She was running over the playing fields. Apparently, someone dumped a whole load of rubbish in the long grass. She was caught up in some barbed wire. She cut her leg pretty badly and fractured her ankle, but Mrs Wheeler says she’ll be OK. She wants you to warn everyone, though. Make sure they know it’s there. Can you call around your friends?”

“Sure, Mum,” Jason replied. “I’ll wash up and do it now. Is Maya home?”

“No, honey. They kept her in hospital, just for tonight. They’re going to X-ray her ankle tomorrow, just to make sure there wasn’t a break,” his mum replied. Jason nodded.

He walked upstairs blankly, his mind reeling. He’d only just been chatting to Maya and now she was in hospital hurt. Hurt because someone had been selfish and stupid and dumped rubbish. He suddenly felt angry. The playing fields were always a mess; the grass was left too long, people dumped stuff, and lots of the fencing was broken and rotten. Someone had to do something about it. He picked up his phone to start calling his friends and stopped. He was someone. He could do it; he could help sort out the playing field.

With renewed purpose, he picked up the phone and started dialling. After several rings, his best friend Phillip picked up the phone.

“Yo, dude, what up?” Phillip asked.

“Maya was hurt crossing the playing fields tonight,” Jason said.

“Seriously?” Phillip replied, suddenly serious.

“Yeah,” Jason said.

“Well, that sucks. What happened?” Phillip asked, all trace of humour gone.

“She fell over rubbish dumped in the long grass. It’s got to stop, man. We’ve got to tidy it up,” Jason said.

“OK, OK, I’m in. What do you need?” Phillip asked. Jason smiled.

“People, a lawnmower. I guess maybe someone to take the rubbish to the dump,” Jason mused.

“I know a guy with a truck. You want to call Marty. His dad has that maintenance company outside of town. I bet they have a mower,” Phillip said.

“Great idea!” Jason said. He grabbed a pen and a pad of paper from his desk and snapped on his desk lamp, wedging the phone between his shoulder and ear so he could make notes. Within an hour, they had a list of people to call. They divided it between them and agreed to start first thing in the morning.

The next day, straight after breakfast, Jason grabbed his phone and started calling up people on his list. He was surprised by how many were willing to help him out. Many of them had kids that played in the fields and were fed up with the mess too. It was decided to meet up the following Saturday to start the work.

The week passed in a blur of activity. Jason's parents were both very proud of him, and his dad agreed to come by and help mend the fencing. Saturday dawned, and Jason was overwhelmed when he got to the playing fields. Not only had Phillip brought his brother's best friend Dan and his huge truck, but several of Dan's friends had come too. Marty, his father, and some of his staff had turned up with ride-on lawnmowers and strimmers. Best of Jason, Maya and Phillip's friends had arrived too, many with pots of paint and brushes to paint the mended fencing that their parents were fixing.

By the end of the day, the playing fields were unrecognisable. The overgrown grass was cropped short. The fences that had been broken and tired were fixed and brightly painted. The rubbish that had littered the place had been gathered and taken away. The team looked out over the grounds with pride. Jason didn't think he could have felt any better than he did right then until he turned around and saw Maya making her way towards him on her crutches. She smiled brightly.

"Wow," she said, stopping beside him. "This is amazing!"

"You started it," he said, nudging her a little.

She giggled and waved a crutch. “Who would have thought something good would come out of this? Thanks, Jason. I mean it.”

Jason smiled and put an arm over her shoulder, giving her a hug. They looked out over the now spotless playing field, where a game of football had spontaneously started, as the sun began to set.

CHAPTER 4: AN ADVENTURE HIKE

Kade picked his way up the rocky path that wound between the tall green pine trees. The trail wasn't too difficult. He'd chosen it specifically so Ally, his little sister, could manage it. Still, the scenery was amazing. He stopped for a few moments, letting Ally catch up and taking in the views of the mountains off in the distance. The air was fresh and crisp, the sky gloriously blue, and the sun just nicely warm. It was a perfect day. Kade smiled as Ally stepped up beside him and looked out over the vista.

"WOW!" she said.

"Nice, isn't it?" Kade smiled.

"It's amazing!" Ally replied.

"We should have a drink. You need to stay hydrated when we're hiking," Kade said, pulling a water bottle from his rucksack. Ally popped her bag down on the trail, pulled out her own water bottle, and took a long drink.

"Which way do we go now?" Ally asked, looking at the trail. It forked just up ahead. One track led downward, through the trees towards the river, the other ran upward along a rocky ridge.

"Which way do you want to go?" Kade asked. "Either trail is pretty easy going."

Ally looked thoughtful. "I think up. I want to see what the view is like."

"OK," Kade said. He helped her pull her purple backpack back on and started up the incline again.

The trail led upward over some rocky patches and then levelled out. The whole forest was laid out below them. Straight ahead, snow-capped peaks dotted the horizon. Kade stood staring at the mountains. He wondered when he could next go rock climbing there. He hadn't been in a while. He was wondering if his friends were free next weekend when Ally cut into his thoughts.

"Kade, look. What is that?" she asked.

Kade glanced at his sister. She was pointing down through the trees towards the river. Kade looked. Sure enough, something orange was bouncing around in the river close to the shore. Grabbing his backpack, Kade pulled out the binoculars he'd brought so they could spot wildlife and trained them down through the treeline. It took him a few seconds to find the patch of orange, but when he did, he froze. It was a raft, clearly wedged against the bank, upside down. He grabbed his phone out of his bag and crouched down so he was level with Ally.

"Ally, there are people in trouble down there. We need to try to help them, but I need to call for help, alright? I'm going to call, but when we get down there, I'm going to pass the phone to you. You stay on the phone with them no matter what, OK? We should get a signal, even down at the river."

Ally nodded, and Kade punched in the emergency number as they raced down back down the trail towards the fork. Kade tried to keep the pace up while making sure Ally was safe. Someone answered the phone.

"Emergency services, how can I help you?" a female voice asked.

"Hi, I'm Kade Duffy. I'm seventeen, hiking the Western Pass trail with my sister. She's twelve. We've seen a raft in trouble on the river below the high point."

“OK, Kade. My name’s Hope. We’re sending help. Can you give us any more information? Is anyone hurt?” the lady said.

“I don’t know yet. We’re heading down the trail towards the river now. When we get there, I’ll see if I can help anyone. I have ropes with me for mountain climbing and a first aid kit. I’m going to hand the phone to Ally while I look,” Kade replied.

“OK, Kade, but please make sure you stay safe. We don’t want anyone–”

Shouts of help had reached Kade’s ears, and he cut the lady off. “I hear people shouting for help. We’re nearly there. Ally, take the phone and stay back from the water.”

Kade handed Ally the phone and sprinted towards the water, pulling his bag off as he went. From the river’s edge, he could make out a few people clinging to the edge of the raft, pinned between it and the rocks. The raft was stopping them from floating away downstream but also stopping them from reaching the shore. The rock would be hard to climb if you were cold and wet.

“Hey,” Kade called.

“Help!” a girl’s voice yelled. “Help us, please.”

Kade pulled out his climbing gear and secured himself to a rock outcrop before cautiously inching out onto the rock the raft had snagged on. From there, he could see three heads in the water.

“Is there anyone else?” he asked.

A girl looked up at him from below, followed by two boys. One of them shouted back. “Carla, she’s stuck under the raft.”

Kade looked back over at Ally. “Ally, tell them four people, one stuck under the raft.”

Ally nodded, and Kade looked down. They all looked cold. He wondered how long they’d been stuck there.

“OK. Let’s get you out first. What’s your name?” he asked the girl.

“Quinn,” she replied as Kade used the ropes to help him get down the slick rocks. He noticed she had a buckle on the front of her life vest. Once he reached her, Kade helped haul her up onto the rock next to him. She was shaking so much she could barely grip onto the rope.

“OK, Quinn. I’m going to put this clip on your life vest. It’ll attach you to me and the rope, OK?” She nodded as Kade clipped her onto the rope.

Carefully and slowly, he helped her inch her way towards the riverbank. Once there, he unclipped her and went back for the next boy. As he did, he saw Ally out of the corner of his eye. She was helping the girl towards some stones further away from the water.

“Who’s next?” Kade asked.

“Nathan,” one boy said, pushing the other forward. “He banged his head, and he’s colder than me. I’ll stay and help Carla.”

Kade nodded and helped Nathan up onto the rope, clipping him in as he had Quinn. Nathan was much less responsive than she had been. Kade realised he had hurt his arm. It took several minutes to reach the shore, but they did, and Kade handed over Nathan to Ally. He was surprised to see she had lit a small fire on a dirt patch near some rocks. He smiled. All those wilderness walks and camps were paying off. He went back over the rocks to where the last boy and Carla were still waiting.

“Hey,” he called.

“Hey, I’m Marty,” the boy said.

“OK, how do we help your friend?” Kade asked.

“We need to tip the raft over, but I don’t know. Carla’s been quiet for a while and I don’t want her to be dragged away,” the boy said.

Kade suddenly had an idea. He looked at Marty, who seemed to be coping the best of all.

“Carla?” Kade yelled. “Can you hear me?”

A muffled, frightened “Yes.” Came from under the boat.

“Carla, can you prod the raft, show me where you are?”

Something moved the top of the raft close to Marty. “Can you dive under the raft?”

“No! Too strong,” she shouted.

Kade was starting to worry, but just then the sound of voices reached him. The rescue team had arrived. Kade felt a wash of relief flood over him.

“Here!” he called, waving. “Over here.”

Kade helped Marty up onto the rope, and they inched back to the riverbank to meet up with the team.

“Well done, young man,” one of them said.

“There’s still a girl, trapped under the raft,” Kade said.

The team rushed forward to help while Kade sat Marty down by Ally’s fire. One of the team members started checking the rafters over, wrapping them in foil blankets and giving them a warm drink. Soon enough, Carla joined them. The rescue team then helped them along to a spot where they could land a helicopter that could take them out of the forest. As Kade and Ally watched the rafters being loaded onto the chopper and flown away, they both felt very proud. When they got home, their story was even on the news. They watched it with their parents in their living room, eating a special takeout meal their dad had bought for his two rescuers.

CHAPTER 5: THE ROCK

Richard laughed as his friends Tony and John raced each other along the road on their bikes. He rode more slowly behind them, taking in the view out over the ocean and feeling the warm sun on his face and arms.

"Dude, come on!" John shouted. He and Tony pulled up in a lay-by and waited for Richard to catch up.

"Yeah, slow or what?" Tony asked.

"Come on. guys. It's not a race," Richard said as he pulled up.

"Good thing too," John huffed.

"This is about your arm, isn't it?" Tony said sympathetically.

"No," Richard said, but even as he did, he knew it was a lie. He'd hurt his arm rock climbing a year ago. It had healed, but he worried about hurting it again. In fact, he hadn't climbed since. He had thought about trying again, and he'd even gone to a climbing wall to try, thinking it would be easier than on real rock. He couldn't do it. He froze up. All he could think about was the accident. Falling, the pain in his arm. He still had all his kit in the bags strapped to his bike. Somehow, he couldn't face taking them off, but he couldn't face the rock either. Richard shook his head to clear his thoughts. Suddenly, he didn't feel like biking up the point anymore.

"Look, you guys go ahead. I think I'm going to go back down to the beach," he said.

"No way, man," John said. "We are going to the point and you are coming with us. You might not climb it, but we can look out over it and chill."

"Yeah, come on," Tony pushed.

Richard sighed. "Fine!"

They started off up the road towards the point. The road spiralled upward, bending around and hugging the coastline. As they peddled around one bend, they noticed a crowd up ahead, looking over the white guard rail and talking all at once. A police car pulled up just as they did, and the officers jumped out and rushed over to the edge.

"Down there!" a woman said. "He slipped and fell."

The boys parked their bikes and walked over, wondering what was going on. An older man was standing at the edge of the crowd, looking worried.

"What happened?" asked Tony.

"A kid slid down the cliff. He's on a ledge halfway down," the man replied.

One of the police officers ran back to the car and frantically picked up his radio. “We’re going to need full rescue. No, no, the helicopter won’t help, we need climbers.”

Tony nudged Richard, who shrugged and said, “The police have climbers.”

The second officer arrived back at the car. “How long, Bill?”

“Too long. That kid’s getting tired, and it’s at least an hour before the team can get here,” the other officer replied.

Richard felt his friends’ eyes on him, but he ignored them. He walked closer to the cliff edge and glanced over. On a small ledge far below was a boy of about eight or nine. He looked terrified, and Richard suddenly felt bad. The climb really wasn't that difficult, and he'd done it before. Right then, he knew he had a choice. He could stay as part of the crowd and hope that the kid was alright for an hour until the rescue climbers arrived or he could do something. Part of him was scared. He was worried about his accident, about falling again. Then he looked down at the kid on the ledge, so scared and alone. An hour would feel like an eternity to him. Richard swallowed hard. He knew what he had to do.

He turned back and walked over to the cops. "I'm a climber," he said.

The officers both looked him up and down, unconvinced. "How old are you son?" one asked.

"Sixteen. Just," Richard replied. "But I've done this climb before and I have my gear."

"I don't know about this," the officer said.

"It's an hour, Bill. I say we let him try. At least he can take some water down to the kid," said the other.

Shortly after, Richard found himself getting his gear from his bike. He rounded up Tony and John and gave them instructions to help him. Richard stepped up to the cliff and took a few deep breaths. He could do this, that kid needed him. He stepped over the railing and slowly made his way down the rock face. He could feel himself panic a little, but every time he felt afraid, he thought about how the kid must be feeling and kept going. Slowly but surely, he made his way to the ledge. He felt a huge relief when his foot touched the solid rock of the ledge. The boy looked terrified but very relieved to see him.

"Hey. I'm Richard, what's your name?" Richard said.

"J-James," said the boy.

Richard carefully helped secure James into a harness so that he'd be safe should he fall, then gave him some water and calmed him down. He checked James over. Surprisingly, he seemed OK apart from a few scratches.

“Can you get me down?” James asked once he’d had a drink.

“Sure, sure, we’ll get you down,” Richard replied.

Richard helped secure James to the ropes, and they slowly began to descend towards the beach. The cops had already driven to the base of the cliff with James’s parents, who were nervously waiting as they landed on the soft sand and Richard unclipped him. As James ran to his parents, Richard sank down and sat on the sand. He’d done it. He’d helped to save James, and he’d also overcome his fear and climbed again. He was so overwhelmed by everything, he felt like he could cry. The police officers were congratulating him and James’s parents were thanking him, but everything seemed a blur.

James was checked over in the local hospital but was totally fine. He really wants to learn to climb now, and Richard has offered to teach him. He’s hoping that taking small steps to teach James will help him get over his accident. Plus, he now has a new friend in James to go climbing with too.

CHAPTER 6: WHO'S AFRAID OF THE DARK?

Mason stared out of his bedroom window at the setting sun. The low autumn light shone off the oranges and reds of the fall leaves and danced across the street over the pumpkins the Watkins had put out next door. His own father had pulled their Halloween decorations out of the garage earlier that evening, and he was looking forward to spending the next day putting them up.

Halloween was one of Mason's favourite times of the year. He loved the fall colours and jumping in the dry leaves. The crisp, cool mornings and hopefully warm afternoons. Best of all though was Halloween. Trick or treat, dressing up, and the local Halloween festival. It was the highlight of the year, a whole afternoon of fun and games followed by a party and the haunted house. Mason loved the afternoon activities, but one thing always made him sad; he never went to the party or the haunted house. Not because they were creepy; he was alright with the fake vampires and spooky ghost props. No, his problem was the dark. He hated it. Even at bedtime, he still needed his nightlight to feel happy and safe. It had never really been a problem before, but this year was different. This year, all of his friends were going to the haunted house after the festival, and a few were even allowed to go to the party.

Mason sighed and slipped off the box seat and flopped on his bed. The sun had almost set and long shadows were reaching up his bedroom wall, threatening to turn dusk into night. How was he ever going to enjoy the festival on Saturday if he couldn't do the haunted house? He started to think it might be better if he didn't go to the festival at all. Maybe he could pretend to be sick or something. Better that than embarrassing himself, right? But then he'd miss the pumpkin rolling contest, and he had the best pumpkin this year. He'd not be able to do the maize maze either. Mason sighed loudly.

"What's up?"

Mason glanced over and saw his brother standing in the doorway. Rob was two years older than Mason and never afraid of anything. Mason rolled over to look at Rob, flicking the lamp on as he did.

"Thinking about the festival," he said quietly. "Everyone is going to the house this year."

"It's awesome! You'll love it," Rob said. He stepped into Mason's room and sat down on his bed. "What's the problem?"

"It'll be dark," Mason said so quietly Rob nearly didn't hear him.

"Still scared, huh?" Rob asked.

Mason nodded. "I want to go, but..." he trailed off, glancing over his shoulder to the window and the darkened sky.

"OK. We can do this," Rob said.

"How?" Mason asked.

"Well, let's start by trying to sleep in the dark tonight," Rob said. "I'll stay in your room if you want."

"Really?" Mason asked, smiling. Rob nodded.

That night, Rob made up a camp bed in Mason's room and they settled down together. Mason turned out the light and tried to sleep, but even with Rob in his room, he felt nervous. His heart beat quickly, and he pulled the blankets high up to his chin. Every noise or shadow made him jump and start. After what seemed like hours, he was still awake, but he did slowly drift off to sleep. The following morning, Rob asked him how he felt. Mason thought about it.

"It was OK with you here, but..." Mason trailed off.

"OK, it's a start. But I have a better idea," Rob said with a smile.

"What?" Mason asked.

Mason sat in the snug with Rob, surrounded by boxes of costumes and craft supplies they'd asked their mother for. Mason wasn't sure how they could help him with his fear of the dark, but he was willing to find out.

"OK," Rob said. "The thing is, I don't think you are afraid of the dark–"

"I am!" Mason cut him off.

"Just listen, bro," Rob said. "I think you're afraid of what you think is in the dark. You overthink everything when you're on your own in the dark. That's why the light helps."

"So, how will this help?" Mason asked, pulling out an old pumpkin costume from a box.

"We're going to sort you out a cool costume that will light up your night," Rob said.

"I don't get it," Mason said, confused.

Rob spent the next few hours helping Mason find the perfect costume. They tried on everything they had and came up with ideas. Rob suggested an angler fish, with a penlight torch as a light. They laughed together at the sight of Mason with the torch stuck to his head. They almost thought they had it with him dressed as a villager complete with a fake light-up burning torch and Rob dressed as Frankenstein's monster, but then they'd have to stay together all night and Rob had plans. They sat down surrounded by a mess of costumes, paper, and fabric. Absently, Mason picked up a string of green battery-powered fairy lights and flicked them on. The end of the string was stuck under a pile of white fabric that lit up with a green, eerie glow. Rob looked over at Mason and smiled.

"I've got it!" he said.

An hour later, Mason found himself standing in front of the hall mirror. The white fabric had been cut and stuck here and there to make a great ghostly shape.

"Light it up," Rob said excitedly.

Mason flicked on the fairy lights, and the whole costume lit up with a bright green glow. It was so cool, but also so bright. Mason smiled.

"One walking nightlight," Rob said. "Let's test it out."

"How?" Mason asked.

"Basement!" they said together.

Mason walked down the basement steps into the darkness. He was usually terrified of going down there with the lights off, but he could see pretty well in his costume. It worked. He wasn't scared at all. He could do this.

On Saturday afternoon, Mason and Rob headed out to the festival. It was lovely and warm, and the leaves were dry and crunchy underfoot. The whole festival looked amazing. Carved pumpkins were dotted around the field. Hay bales were stacked up here and there to use as seats. A huge sign above the entrance to part of the field said *Maize Maze* in red letters. Two scarecrows were standing under it, welcoming people in. Little kids were running around laughing and shouting, and a few people were setting up an enormous BBQ grill.

Mason tackled the maze and had great fun winding through the trails, jumping at the scary models that had been hidden here and there throughout. Every jump ended in laughter. After the maze, he and Rob met up and had things from the BBQ, then headed over to the pumpkin rolling contest.

The contest was just about to start when they arrived. They spent a while watching the pumpkins rolling down the ramp and waiting to see which pumpkin would make it. They stayed there until the sun sank low in the sky. The other kids started to head home when the last pumpkin rolled down the ramp and the winner was announced.

Mason suddenly started to feel more concerned as the sun set and darkness started to settle around them. The park became quiet as everyone headed home or to go trick-or-treating. Mason hurried off with his friends to do some trick-or-treating before the haunted house opened. As he walked past the haunted house, done up all spooky, he shuddered. For the first time, he wondered if the lights in his costume would be enough.

A short while later, Mason was back at the haunted house. He was starting to feel afraid again. The dark seemed to close in around him. He took a deep breath as the other kids surged towards the door of the house, then he turned on his lights and headed to the door too.

Inside, he found the house was lighter than he had thought. He followed his friends through the rooms. Some had creepy dioramas set up, others had pictures whose eyes followed you or animatronic creatures that cackled and moved. It was brilliant. Some of the rooms had real people in them, dressed up in costumes, who jumped out at him when he walked in. Mason screamed a few times, but he laughed afterwards. He forgot that it was dark and simply enjoyed the house. His friends laughed together as they rushed from room to room.

Later that night, Mason lay on his bed thinking about all the fun he'd had. Maybe Rob had been right. He wasn't afraid of the dark. He overthought it. Without a word, he reached over and knocked off the lamp. Then, he lay back and thought about all the fun he'd had until he fell fast asleep, alone and in the dark.

CHAPTER 7: LIVE THE DREAM

Ethan smudged the charcoal a little over the eyebrow he had just sketched on his drawing pad. He breathed the fresh air deeply and glanced back at the girl he'd chosen to sketch, sitting on a bench a few feet away. She was looking out over the lake in the park, unaware he even existed, but that didn't matter. Ethan just loved sketching. People, places, animals. Anything really, he just loved to draw.

He spent the rest of the afternoon in the park sketching things. He was pretty good, even if he said so himself. Ethan trudged home reluctantly. He loved his family, but his dad really wanted him to focus on things in school he didn't like. It wasn't that he didn't understand it was important to learn about maths and science, just that he was only OK at them and he loved art. It was what he wanted to do more than anything in the world, but he never said anything to his father. It made him a little sad.

Ethan put his sketchbook in his room and headed down for dinner. His mum, dad, and sister were already sitting at the table, but he was surprised to see two other places set out.

"Hey," Ethan said. "Who's coming to dinner?"

"Me, kid."

Ethan looked up as his grandfather walked in.

"Grandpa!" Ethan rushed over and hugged his grandfather.

They all sat down and ate dinner together. Grandpa told lots of fun stories, and everyone seemed to be having a good time until they started talking about school. Ethan's sister Evelyn was fine chatting about her grades and how well things were going for her in school, but that wasn't the same for Ethan. He grew very quiet.

"So, Ethan, aren't you going to tell your grandpa how well school's going?" his dad asked.

"Er, sure, it's fine I guess," Ethan replied.

"Are you sure?" Grandpa asked.

"Well, he has been focusing more on proper subjects this year," his father said, though his grandfather looked confused.

"Yeah," Ethan replied, pushing his veggies around his plate. "Can I be excused?"

"Sure," his mother said.

Ethan left the table and rushed upstairs. He was busy sketching again when his grandfather knocked on the door and came in. He crossed over the room and sat down as Ethan closed his sketchbook and pushed it away. It was what he always did when someone came into his room. His father never really liked to see him sketching. Then again, his father was never really interested in what was in the books, unlike his grandfather.

His grandpa reached over and picked up the book in silence. He flicked through the pages, nodding as he did so.

"You did these?" he asked.

Ethan nodded. "Yeah, look, Grandpa, I know I need to focus on other things, but I love to draw."

"You don't need to convince me, kid. These are good," Grandpa said.

"Really?" Ethan asked.

"Really," Grandpa replied. "Can I take this?"

"Er, sure," Ethan replied.

Grandpa took the sketchbook with him and left Ethan alone and confused. He didn't think much more about the sketches until the next day when his grandpa snuck into his room again, smiling secretly as he closed the door.

"I sent your sketches," he whispered with a big smile.

"Sent them where?" asked Ethan, suddenly alarmed.

"To my friend Miriam. She's a big deal in the art world. She told me about this competition for teen artists, so I sent her your sketches."

Ethan started to sweat. He couldn't believe it. "Grandpa, why did you do that?"

"Because you're good. What's the problem?"

Ethan wasn't sure what to say. He shook his head slowly. "Dad will be annoyed. He doesn't want me doing art. He says focusing on it is silly. No one ever made a living as an artist."

"Hey, you might be an artist, maybe not, but you should always try to follow your dreams. You have no idea where they can take you, and you have real talent. Even Miriam said so. You know Miriam wanted to be an artist. She studied art, and she's pretty good at it. Now she's not an artist, but she still enjoys painting and she runs a very successful art gallery."

Ethan had never thought about that. Maybe he should focus more on his art but keep his other studies going too. Perhaps his father wouldn't flip out if he thought Ethan was pursuing a dream to work in the art industry like Miriam.

"Come on, kid," Grandpa said.

"Where are we going?" Ethan asked.

"To the city. I think you should meet Miriam," Grandpa replied.

Ethan followed his grandpa downstairs and grabbed his coat. His father came out of the kitchen and frowned at them as Grandpa pulled on his coat.

"Where are you two off to?" Dad asked.

"The city, see a lady about a painting," Grandpa said.

"Dad." Ethan's father sighed, exasperated. "I don't want you filling Ethan's head with fantasies about painting."

"Hey, you should see his drawings. They're really good. Besides, I'm taking the boy to see my friend Miriam. She owns her own art gallery. Made a fortune. You're telling me that isn't a good job for someone?" Grandpa said.

Ethan's father huffed, but he waved his paper at the door and muttered something about having work to do.

Ethan spent the day in the city with his grandfather and Miriam. It was amazing. They saw artworks at the museum and then more at Miriam's gallery. She told him all about how she had come to do what she did and even offered to let him intern for her during the summer holidays to learn more. The more he saw of the art gallery and the paintings, the more he wanted to paint and sketch.

He got home that night enthusiastic about everything. He told his mother about all the wonderful things he'd seen, the paintings, and the gallery. She seemed pleased he was so upbeat and happy, but his father looked less impressed.

"And, Mum, she offered me an internship for the holidays," Ethan concluded.

"Well, you won't be taking it will you?" his father suddenly put in.

Ethan felt his face fall. "Why? I won't ask you to drive me or anything. I can get the bus."

"Nonsense. You can stay with me, come home on weekends. We'll have a great time," Grandpa said.

"Transport isn't the issue. I thought you were going to intern with me at the office. A proper internship," his father said.

"Charles," his mother said. "I think Ethan should be allowed to choose himself."

Ethan's father looked irritated, but he simply nodded his agreement. Ethan spent the next few days trying to decide what to do about the internship. Although he knew he wanted to work with Miriam, he just couldn't work out how to do that without annoying his father.

The next weekend, Grandpa turned up unexpectedly, and he wasn't alone. Grandpa burst through the door with Miriam in tow, waving an envelope.

"You won, kid!" he said to Ethan.

"Won what?" Mum asked.

"The Teen Artist Award. First place," Miriam said with a smile.

"You entered a competition?" Dad asked sternly.

Ethan suddenly felt proud. He turned to face his dad. "Grandpa did it. He entered my sketches. And I won. Dad, I know you want me to do well. I know you worry I won't make anything of myself if I pursue art. But if I don't? If I don't try at least, then I'll really be a failure. I want to do what Miriam did. I want to study art and have a fall-back position just like she did. I want to do her internship."

Surprisingly, his father smiled. "OK."

"OK?" Ethan replied.

"Yes. You never showed any fire before. Never stood up for what you wanted. If you can't do that, then you give up. If you have fire and passion, then you'll follow up on it." Dad smiled.

Ethan was stunned. A smile spread over his face, then he ran up to his dad and hugged him.

"Hey, let's celebrate!" Grandpa said. "Get in the car. We're going out. My treat."

Everyone rushed out to the car happily. Ethan paused at the doorway, though, taking a moment to appreciate that the world had opened up before him. His dreams were one step closer to becoming real, and he liked the feeling. He liked it a lot.

DISCLAIMER

This book contains opinions and ideas of the author and is meant to teach the reader informative and helpful knowledge while due care should be taken by the user in the application of the information provided. The instructions and strategies are possibly not right for every reader and there is no guarantee that they work for everyone. Using this book and implementing the information/recipes therein contained is explicitly your own responsibility and risk. This work with all its contents, does not guarantee correctness, completion, quality, or correctness of the provided information. Misinformation or misprints cannot be completely eliminated.